THE ADVENTURES OF

Captain Pugwash

™

The Vanishing Ship

RED FOX

A Red Fox Book

Published by Random House Children's Books
20 Vauxhall Bridge Road, London SW1V 2SA

A division of The Random House Group Ltd
London Melbourne Sydney Auckland
Johannesburg and agencies throughout the world

The Adventures of Captain Pugwash
Created by John Ryan
© Britt Allcroft (Development) Limited 2000
All rights worldwide Britt Allcroft (Development) Limited
CAPTAIN PUGWASH is a trademark of Britt Allcroft (Development) Limited
THE BRITT ALLCROFT COMPANY is a trademark of The Britt Allcroft Company plc

Cover illustration by Ian Hillyard
Inside illustrations by Red Central Limited

Text adapted by Sally Byford from the original TV story

1 3 5 7 9 10 8 6 4 2

THE RANDOM HOUSE GROUP Limited Reg. No. 954009

www.randomhouse.co.uk

ISBN 0 09 940817 1

Captain Pugwash and his crew were returning to the
harbour after a busy day's shopping in Portobello.
They were ready to load up the Black Pig and sail off
on another seafaring adventure. But back at the harbour,
they got a horrible shock – the Black Pig had vanished!

Tom pointed out to sea. "Look, Captain, there's our ship!"

"Shuddering shellfish!" wailed Pugwash. "Cut-throat Jake's on board. He's taken the Black Pig! Come back!"

"What shall we do?" moaned the Mate, as the Black Pig disappeared into the distance.

Tom had been thinking hard. "I've got an idea," he said. "Jake and his crew are all on our ship, so why don't we take their ship."

Pugwash sighed. "I suppose the Flying Dustman is better than nothing," he said.

On board the Black Pig, Cut-throat Jake and his crew were celebrating their victory.

"This will be the end of that old fool Pugwash," chuckled Jake. "Whoever heard of a pirate without a ship!"

Dook, Swine and Stinka roared with laughter.

Captain Pugwash and his crew had found the Flying Dustman. Jake had left two men to guard the ship, but they were already fast asleep. Tom, Willy, Jonah and the Mate leapt on board, and pushed them into the sea.

Then Pugwash strode onto the ship feeling much happier.

"What's next, Captain?" asked Tom. "Shall we follow the Black Pig?"

"I was going to say that," said Pugwash. And off they sailed.

While his crew was busy on deck, Captain Pugwash searched for treasure in Cut-throat Jake's cabin.

At first he was disappointed. All he could find were boxes of old rubbish. Then he stumbled upon a large wooden chest. Quickly, Pugwash opened it up. Inside were hundreds of glittering gold doubloons.

"Stuttering starfish! I'm rich!" he cried.

At that moment, Tom peeped round the door. "Captain," he called, "the Black Pig…" Then Tom saw the treasure. "Wow!" he gasped.

Pugwash slammed the lid shut. "What is it?" he said crossly.

"The Black Pig's in sight," said Tom. "Hurry!"

Pugwash rushed up on deck and saw the Black Pig ahead.

"Are we going to attack, Captain?" asked Jonah.

"We can't harm the Black Pig," said Pugwash. "Let's wait and see what Jake does first."

Jake was furious when he saw Captain Pugwash on the
Flying Dustman, but he didn't want to attack his ship, either.
"We'll wait and see what that old fool does first," he said.

By evening, Pugwash and Jake were getting tired of waiting
and they both decided to go to bed.

Soon everyone on the Black Pig and the Flying Dustman had
fallen asleep. All except for Tom. He was busy planning to get
the Black Pig back. Secretly, he drew two identical maps, and
on each map he marked a cross on Buccaneer Island. Tom
knew there wasn't any treasure there, but he wanted Jake and
the Captain to think there was.

Then Tom tip-toed into Cut-throat Jake's cabin, where Pugwash was asleep and snoring loudly. He put one of the maps on the floor by the bed so Pugwash would see it in the morning.

"Now for the other map," he whispered to himself, as he crept quietly away.

No one saw Tom as he rowed over to the Black Pig, tied up the boat and climbed aboard.

Tom went straight to Pugwash's cabin, where Jake was sleeping. He wanted Jake to wake up so he opened the bed curtains with a loud rattle.

Jake woke up immediately. "What are you doing here? And what's that you've got?" he growled.

"It belongs to the Captain," said Tom. "He sent me to fetch it."

Jake snatched the map. "So Pugwash has buried his treasure on Buccaneer Island," he snarled. "We'll sail there at once, and you're coming with us!"

The next morning, Pugwash was woken by the clatter of Jake's alarm clock. He fell out of bed with a bump and landed right beside the map that Tom had left on the floor. "I've never seen this before," he said, sitting up to get a closer look. "Doddering dolphins. It must be Jake's treasure map!"

Pugwash rushed on deck to share the good news with his crew. "Jake's treasure is buried on Buccaneer Island," he shouted, waving the map. "Which way do we go, Tom?"

There was no answer. Willy, Jonah and the Mate searched the ship, but Tom was nowhere to be found.

"The Black Pig's disappeared, too," the Mate said suddenly. "Where's it gone?"

"Don't ask stupid questions," said Pugwash. "When we find this treasure, we can buy a new Black Pig."

Tom was on Buccaneer Island with Cut-throat Jake and his crew. Dook, Swine and Stinka were digging as fast as they could while Jake roared orders at them.

"Dig deeper, you fools," he shouted.

Tom kept very quiet and waited until they had forgotten all about him. Then he crept away, quickly untied the boat and rowed back to the Black Pig.

The Flying Dustman had almost reached Buccaneer Island
when Pugwash and his crew saw the Black Pig coming straight
towards them.

"Help!" wailed Pugwash. "It could be a trick!"

Willy looked through his telescope. "There's Tom at the
wheel!" he cried in amazement.

"Juddering jellyfish! What's he doing?" said Pugwash.

When the two ships were side by side, Tom waved at the crew on the Flying Dustman. "There's no treasure on the island," he shouted. "Jake has already looked. But remember what you found in his cabin, Captain. Now you can take it."

"Oh yes," said Pugwash. "I forgot to say. There's a large chest in Jake's cabin. Can you move it to the Black Pig?"

On Buccaneer Island, Dook, Swine and Stinka had given up digging. They hadn't found any treasure and Cut-throat Jake was furious. He was even angrier when he saw his treasure chest being moved from the Flying Dustman to the Black Pig.

He jumped up and down with rage. "That old fool Pugwash has got my rowing boat, my Black Pig, my Flying Dustman – and now he's got my treasure!" he roared.

Jake's treasure chest was soon safely stowed away in Pugwash's cabin. Then the Captain and his crew let the Flying Dustman drift away and boarded their own ship once more.

As they set sail for Portobello, they looked back at Buccaneer Island and waved cheerfully at Cut-throat Jake. If Jake wanted the Flying Dustman back, he'd have to swim for it!